For Aunt Janet —S.L.
For Hannes —M.L.

GRUMPY MONKEY
PARTY TIME!

By Suzanne Lang

Illustrated by Max Lang

Random House 🏠 New York

One perfectly pleasant afternoon,
Jim Panzee found an invitation on his branch.

"Party?" said Jim. "Hmmm . . ."

"It'll be a great time," said Norman from next door. "We can dance—"

"Dance?" Jim exclaimed, cutting Norman off. "I can't dance!"

"Everyone can dance," said Hyena.
"Come on, show us your moves."

"I don't have any moves," said Jim.
"Sure you do," said Hyena. "You
just need to try."

So Jim tried to dance.

"You should have taken him at his word," Norman said to Hyena.

"If Jim doesn't know how to dance," said Oxpecker, "we'll just have to teach him."

Everyone was excited to teach Jim how to dance.
"You've got to feel the beat," the lizards said.

"You've got to strut your stuff," said Ostrich.

"You've got to shake your butt," said the baboons.

"He's doing it! He's dancing!" everyone cheered.

"Party time!" said Norman.
And they headed to Porcupine's party.

At the party, everyone wanted to dance with Jim.

"Dance with us!" said the ground squirrels.

"Care to shake a tail feather?" asked Peacock.

"May we cut in?" asked the warthogs.

"Me next!" said Rhino.
Jim danced and danced.
Everyone on the dance floor
was having a great time.
Everyone except Jim.

"Isn't this the best?" chirped Oxpecker.

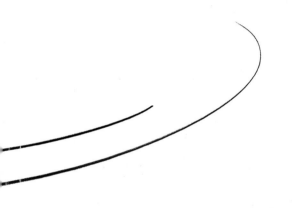

And then it got worse.

"No!" Jim said. "This is not the best! It's the worst! I don't like dancing!"

The other animals stared in amazement.

"Who ever heard of someone who doesn't like dancing?" asked Oxpecker.

"Actually," said Water Buffalo,
"I don't like dancing, either. But
I never said anything because
I thought I was the only one."

"I know others enjoy themselves, but I
always feel silly on the dance floor. I'd rather
do something else," squawked Marabou.

"To be honest," chimed in Bat, "dance floors are always too loud for my taste."

"I'm going home," Jim said. And he turned to go . . .

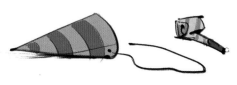

. . . and bumped smack into Norman!

"You're not leaving, are you?"
asked Porcupine.

"Everyone at this party wants to dance," said Jim, "but we don't like dancing."

"It's not for everyone," Norman agreed.

"But now I'll have too much food," said Porcupine sadly.

"Oh, Porcupine, we didn't mean to upset you. . . ." Jim paused. "Wait. There's food at this party?"

And, indeed, there was lots of wonderful food.

And plenty of games, too.

And so they stayed at the party.

Jim enjoyed the wonderful food. He laughed
with his friends. He even played a game or two.

But he did not dance.

It was a great time.